GOLDEN OOJAMAFLIPS

A collection of short stories

Volume 17

MIKE PEARCE

DEDICATION

This book is dedicated to all those in lockdown due to the
pandemic of 2020

CONTENTS

ACKNOWLEDGEMENTS

The author would like to thank Christine Pearce
for reading and checking through the manuscript.

PREVIEW

Behind each short story in this volume there is
always a light emerging out of the darkness. A
chance that things will change for the better. Be
it coming out of poverty or even a tree losing all
its leaves only to produce even more the next
spring. This volume had as wide variety of
different stories form wedding dresses to
mulberry trees

1 MOTHER LOSES LEAVES

Mother was moved by the strong wind. Her branches moved up and down as if dancing to a lively song. The wind swept like waves along the fronts of evergreen bushes. The whole tree was bright green with leaves but was now golden yellow; the children had given all back to her before leaving.

Her children grew up together from little buds leaves became closer touching they shared the same water source and sugars as the others. They felt the same rain, the same sunshine and dew in the same air

Mother said to them, "Stay with me as though it's the last day in the world." They were trying to grip tightly with their thin stalks. Every leaf is fiercely shaken to death at the same time. The mother looked on to see which ones were leaving.

"I'm leaving, goodbye mother," as one leaf was suddenly thrown off hitting the ground. Some hung on their edges battered and torn. All will not have enough green to capture the last pack of energy from the sun. Now they were all being shaken very fast. Like a seizure. Some would hang on until spring, brown and shrivelled, mother rocked and rocked again.

The warm wind removed the last of the water and made their fine surface hard, dry and rigid. Many moved together in the gusts of winds like little flags on bunting.

Those that stood high on the top of the tree with a lot of light were lost first. No bird dare stay on the tree all insects that fed on the leaves had long gone. Leaves fell to be squashed, tangled in a pile of wetness as the mother watched. Sadly more and more of her children were lost. What was the use of her being there, her seeds could never grow on the tarmac below. Some of her children stuck to car windows only to be flicked off when the wipers moved others were captured like fish in a net on wire netting. The mother was used to losing her children every year, her leaves mingling with those from other trees.

Her next children were waiting inside the buds. Mother was not fully grown but lichens and dirt covered the trunk and branches. There was nobody to grieve for her, console or hug her.

She was now naked her trunk and branches exposed to the oncoming winter elements. Her fear was that if she grew too big she would lose many branches and even be chopped down. Now she was sleeping her circulation shut down but her roots were still able to grow. Rain would fall and if it was very freezing all her surface would be coated in ice. Frost would also cover her like a layer of icing

What was she for? What is her purpose? Did they put her there to keep green campaigners happy so that the area was not totally built up? Was it to remind people of what the countryside was like and rekindle childhood experiences?

She would rather be in a wood with all the wildlife and protection like her ancient family.

Not to be a display item, a small human idol stuck in the centre of a car park. "Damn you all," she said I am a prisoner held in a life sentence for today and tomorrow. She looked and saw a girl holding one of her children tightly, her blond hair blowing across the surface. Was she waiting for someone or something?

Her hands were tucked under the jumper sleeves, she was sitting on the end of the curb a baby cried in the distance but she did not look up holding the stem she twirled the leaf round and round to see the golden colour. A child holding his mother's hand walked past in a yellow hooded plastic mac. It looked at the girl and thinks why is she playing with a leaf in her hand. The mother removed the mac hugged her baby and puts her into the car. The tree looks on wishing she could have held her children and watched them grow. The wind blew and more leaves fly past like a stream in front of her. She picked up another one. The girl was still holding the two leaves she left and put them in her pocket

2 MOTHERS OF FERTILITY

Most life was brief and food often short but they survived. They clung onto their beliefs. Belief that the mother of fertility, mother earth from which everything arose, would provide abundant crops and children that grew up like their crops. She had always provided before and the miracle of birth shone in the eyes of people especially women. All life came from the womb of mother earth. She would nurture and sustain everyone through her body.

But many forgot about her and took everyday living for granted and disasters happened so it was decided that the stone carvers should represent her as very small amulets and as huge figures just like those found representing the kings of Egypt. These statues all had massive swollen legs and upper arms with tiny feet and huge buttocks.

To create a place of pilgrimage they needed a temple and underground chambers attended by these large women. Built by men it needed to be managed by those in the community who were female and large. In this time it was seen as good, especially for men, for women to be large.

This influenced many families and they decided to feed up their children.

Being large indicated that a woman stored a lot of energy and there was a plentiful food source. From the age of four they would pour buttery milk down their throats most of the day. Girls were given more food than boys and as they grew they would include other foods such as dates, nuts, oil, fatty lamb and goats.

To help promote this, special women called Fatners were responsible for feeding groups of girls. If they were sick they would force them to eat it and beat them if they did not eat their food. The little girls as they grew up became used to drinking and eating. The Fatners even included plant extracts which they believed would fatten them quicker. The parents believed by making their daughters fat they would be real women representative of their fertility god.

Many mothers would even fatten up their girl to be ready for a partner who had showed intent. Both women and especially men at this time revered the rolling layers of skin or the stretch marks on arms and thighs.

 Even older women could be fattened up. Being fat meant that these women as seen in some stone representatives of these gods would be portrayed lying on a couch or sitting which is what these fattened girls would do most of the day. As they aged they would become more tired and weak. They were regarded as beautiful girls and would age quicker and many have children at young ages and even are able to wear adult clothes.

To gain a blessing from their mother of fertility they would sacrifice sheep and goats at the temple. Spirals in shrines indicated eternity, renewal, rebirth and regrowth through ample offspring and new crops. These large girls were made guardians of the temple and feasted on the sacrificed animals afterwards. The statues acted as guardian figures. The adoration of these women meant there was peace and love and no war. Society felt safe from every day misfortunes and disasters and life was good.

3 A GENDER FLUID TREE-
THE MULBERRY

Many of you know my name from the nineteenth century nursery rhyme. Here we go round the mulberry bush on a cold and frosty morning. The subsequent verses encourage children to do tasks which they are not fond of doing. This is the way we wash our face, comb our hair, brush our teeth, put on our shoes etc.

Some suggest the rhyme originated from female prisoners in Wakefield circling round and round a mulberry tree with their children to keep them amused

My name may have been given initially to a bramble bush but that changed I'm happy especially when young and I can withstand dry conditions and little food. I can grow fast but it will take 10 years before fruiting. To some I represent patience as my buds won't open until the cold weather has passed. My fruits can be whites or dark red. Romans ate my berries at feasts.

I've been called the tree of life, the herb of immortality and the tree of gold. Few insects will attack my leaves but as many know the silk worm finds my leaves delicious.

My fruits can be white or dark red. Greek legend says they were once all white. Two lovers Pyramus and Thisbe were forbidden to marry but met secretly under my tree. Thisbe arrived early and sees a lioness so runs into a cave dropping her shawl under the tree. She sees a lioness whose mouth was covered in blood from a recent kill Blood drips onto the shawl. Pyramus arrives at the tree and chases the lion away and sees the blood. He thinks Thisbe has been eaten so he plunges his sword into his belly and dies. Thisbe emerges from the cave and sees her dead lover and in grief falls on the sword herself. The gods are watching and decide to stain the mulberry fruits colour from white to red the colour of blood to honour forbidden love.

My red berries are very attractive to birds and used as a trap crop to attract them away from cherry orchards. They say my berries are slightly hallucigenic and have been used as a protection from disease for over 5000 years. I have an alkaloid which lowers sugar absorbtion reducing diabetes. They say leaves put under a pillow can bring psychic dreams.

Unfortunately I produce a lot of light weight pollen and I am banned in some countries as I am not good for hay fever sufferers.

German folk law suggests the devil polishes his boots with my roots so I am associated with evil.

Beware if you buy me in a garden centre as I may not be all you think. Male flowers cannot make fruit, so there are no seeds or unviable seeds. I am gender fluid throughout the season I can change sex from male to female then back to male again. I can even be both male and female on the same tree, some branches with female flowers, some with male. To be truly male all my flowers must be male and to be female all flowers must be female. Strong light and high temperature may make me male while high humidity female. Perhaps I should fear the onset of global warming.

4 THE GOLDEN CHAMBER

It was raining. The entrance to her workplace was part of an old town wall, once a Norman defence. On each side were the remains of arrow slits which were now sealed up. The ledges now formed perches for restless pigeons which sat on their nests there rearing their young.

When would it stop raining she thought? I wanted to get home, but if I left now I would be soaked and my other dry clothes are inside my washing basket at home. There was a lot of fluttering above her. She looked up at the entrance and saw two pigeons were fighting for a space on a ledge. Bits of old nest were being flung down onto the wet pavement below only to be swept along into the gutter and down the road into the huge drain.

More and more nest material was coming down. Some of it may have been there for many many years. Alice moved to the side. There was a splat and a large piece of compacted nest fell down. She watched as the rain separated the old straw and twigs. Something caught her eye it was something shiny. She stooped down to pick what was left of the remaining straw bundle up and saw it was a button attached to something thin and solid. Brushing off the straw she saw it looked like a little flat leather purse. The leather was very shrivelled and old and torn in places. She half expected it to all fall apart in her hands. Looking at the button it had a small sign on it.

The rain had now stopped. A glimmer of sunshine peeped out from behind the clouds. It would soon dry up as the soil was chalk and it didn't take long to soak into the ground. She took out a carrier bag from her handbag and put the tiny purse at the bottom and hurried long the street towards the underground station. The usual home time rush was in full swing. She hated being jostled and having to push past people especially if they were in groups and when they were pulling cases. She managed to get on the tube straight away and even found a seat. She held her bag close to her until she reached her stop. It started to rain again so she ran from the underground station to her flat, opened the door, went inside and sat down. She remembered the little purse and took out the carrier bag. The leather was stuck tightly together so she decided to dampen it and put the whole purse into a saucer of warm water. She then teased up the inside slowly with a knife. As she did so she could see there was a small piece of parchment inside. She hoped that the water had not damaged any writing that might be on it. She put the purse right under the water and gradually pulled out the parchment, and laid it on a piece of tissue on the table to dry with the purse next to it. She had just decided to go to bed when she again looked at the parchment. She could make out faint writings on it but even with a magnifier she could not read them. There were also lines like a sort of map. She decided that the next day she would copy it as best she could and show it to her friend who was good at translating this kind of thing. She went to bed but her head was spinning round and round. She was dreaming and saw in front of her large circular stones with snake like carvings and two spirals which looked like two large eyes carved into the stone.

The next day was Saturday so she didn't have to go to work. She was still tired, had breakfast and copied the drawings on the parchment and left the house.

She would go and see her friend around the corner. She knocked on the door but there was no reply but she was just about to leave when the door opened.

"Oh it's you," her friend said. "It's early and it's Saturday and usually I lie in but it's ok. I'm a lazy person. Come inside and I'll make some coffee."

They sat around a small table. "Why are you here so early?"

"Well I found something. Just as I was standing outside our office, a whole load of pigeon muck came down from the old walls. In it was what looks like an old purse. It has a button on it. Look. Inside was a piece of parchment and I drew the pattern on it hoping you could help me decipher it

. Her friend looked but did not say anything. "A small piece of parchment?" he said.

She gave him the scrap of paper with the drawing on it. "I thought since you like ancient history you may be able to make sense of it as I can't." Her friend looked at the copy.

"Right, there's a sign for water there, but I don't know what the other figures mean. But there is definitely a map. Look there's a stream or a river and next to it what looks like a small wood and what looks like a pile of stones."

"The only river near here is that small stream at the bottom of the hill. Some say that once it was a river and there are the remains of an oak forest at the top."

"I've been there many times," her friend said "It's a bit rocky it probably was part of a volcano at some time. They say it was once part of a goldmine."

"Let's go." she said.

"Hey wait, its Saturday. I'm not dressed and need a bit of time to get myself together before even thinking of going out. Have another coffee and I'll be back down in ten minutes."

She waited patiently, then the door opened and her friend was there dressed in a red anorak and walking shoes. "I'll just feed the cat then we're off."

They went down the bottom of the hill and followed what was left of the stream up to the top. Perhaps at one time it was a river; there were still willows further back. As they neared the top they could hear the water trickling over stones and bubble downward.

"It's lovely and cool," she said.

"Its good water they bottle it way down at the bottom of the valley."

They carried on looking for the large boulders on the top. Her friend said, "These were probably much larger at one time but have been weathered in the past. Also a plane in the war I believe dropped a packet of bombs her before it returned home. There must have been some sort of communications tower up here at one time."

"Wait. What's that?" and she pointed to a large flat sided rock. On it, but really worn was the carving of a spiral serpent. "Never noticed that before. They say if you have something in your mind you will notice it more."

"Let's go onto the top of it." They pushed back the brambles and got close to the rock. She ran her hand over the circles.

"Look," her friend said. "There's a sort of gulley running on one side of the rock."

They walked down it and behind the rock they saw an opening. "Looks like a cave, shall we go in?" She hesitated as there could be a deep drop just inside and one would not see it as it was very dark.

"It's ok," her friend said, "I have a torch on my phone." So in they went. There were small pools of water inside and the rock was covered in a bright green moss and large ferns were on the walls.

"There must be an opening upwards or these would not grow here." Soon enough they came to an open area and they could see the sky above. Water was dripping down from its side into small pools. It was like a hidden garden.

"Wonder what's on the other side?" They walked over.

She looked at her watch. It had stopped. She picked up her mobile phone but there was no signal. They reached an area where the stone underneath their feet was white.

"It's a layer of quartz," her friend said. "Even the walls are white." There was a narrow slit in the wall at the other end. They hesitated then decided to squeeze through. She thought, what if we got stuck no one would hear us.

On the other side was a wall of water falling down in front of them. They could see through it. There was a huge cavern the size of a cathedral. They rushed through the water and stood looking up at the tall height. They could see gaps where there were openings to the surface and light came through. A few pigeons fluttered around near the openings then left and all was silent. The walls had bands of quartz on them. Her friend ran his hand over them. Look there's something in these quartz bands. She looked. "It's gold. I'm sure it's gold." They managed to pull out several large pieces but then they noticed the walls were covered with what seemed like small grey round protrusions.

"Never seen that before," her friend said. He put his hand on one. "Why it's warm," he said but pulled back as suddenly as the protrusion started to move upwards then remained still. "There's some sort of creature," he said. "Like giant woodlice." They looked round the whole of the cave and saw the walls were covered in them. She said, "I don't like this; they may decide to come at us especially if we tread on one of them."

"Let's carry on," said her friend. "Perhaps well come to an opening to the outside."

On the ground were large tall rocks which they had to walk over and in some cases balance their weight. They were using her friend's torch on his mobile phone. Suddenly she tripped and fell.

"Oh my ankle, I've hurt it." her friend picked her up.

"Can you carry on?" It was no use she could hardly walk especially over this jigsaw of stones.

"Blast," he said, and as he did so they heard scuttling noises. Looking up they saw on the sides of the walls masses of these lump like creatures moving toward' them over the sides of the cave. They could see they were moving down to floor level. She screamed. "They know that I had been hurt and are coming in for the kill." They scuttled nearer to them, hundreds of them, crawling up and over the high rocks. Her friend attempted to throw them off but was bitten. They kept coming and were soon on top of her and she fell to the ground. She could feel them on her chest then she felt a huge pressure on the underside of her body as if they were trying to push through her skin. She wriggled and screamed and passed out. Suddenly her whole body was lifted up above the rocks and she was moving forward like some performer who was being carried forward lifted up lying flat by a line of men.

Where was she going? Her friend tried to grab hold of her but she continued to be moved into the darkness. Her friend could do nothing to stop this. He thought to his horror that they must be moving her perhaps towards a giant one of these creatures a queen who wanted to feed on her.

She was out of the stony area and was put down on a sandy area. Her friend was already there. She had woken.

"Look," he said. They could hear what sounded like lapping waves on rock. "It's the sea and it's coming in, an underground sea. "The creatures that carried you have gone into the waves and are no longer to be seen." They could clearly see the white waves rolling onto the shore. There was even sea weed on the sand. "These caves must go on for miles, he said." We are quite a way from the sea."

"What if the tide comes in? We will be drowned," she said.

"Don't worry; the strand line is quite a distance so it's likely it would not reach us."

"But I don't want to stay here any longer," she said. "I'm cold and scared and my foot hurts."

"Right then let's look for a way out."

They felt around the walls of the cave. "I can feel something," she said. "It's a door but covered in sand." Her friend pulled hard at it and the layer of sand fell away revealing a very narrow passage. Perhaps we'll find some treasure," he said jokingly. At the end of the tunnel they were in a small chamber. The walls of which were covered in gold and shells of all kinds.

"It's a grotto," she said. "Like they made in Victorian times. They used to hold secret meetings in these."

"In that case there must be a way in from the outside." In the corner was a huge bunch of rags they went over to it and removed the top layer. To their horror they could see a skull. There was a person underneath. "Must have been a man guarding this place at one time and he died here still guarding."

They could see that part of the shell wall behind them had no shells. There was another door. This time when they pulled it, it fell flat onto the ground, the hinges had rusted away. They slid past the dead man and found a corridor whose walls had what looked like small bags hanging from rusty hooks. As soon as they touched them they fell to the floor in pieces. "The materials rotted away," she said.

"They must have contained items for wearing at a ceremony," her friend said. They sifted through the fragments on the floor to see if any intact pieces were left or even parchment with writings on.

Her hand hit something hard on the floor. She picked it up and rubbed the rough surface with her hand. It was a brooch with spirals of gold metal surrounding what looked like a red gemstone in the centre. They sifted through the other debris and found several more brooches exactly the same.

They could hear the rumbling of the sea echoing along the corridor.

"I don't like it in here," she said. They went further down the tunnel which led to some steep steps. They could smell the smell of wet soil. "Must be nearing the entrance," her friend said but as he did so the soil walls of the steps started to cave in. She scrambled to the top of the steps. She could see light and put her arm out to try and pull herself up but the soil around her was collapsing inwards. All went black and she couldn't move as if she was in a grave of wet soil.

It was raining. A farmer had wanted to harvest his corn but the window of opportunity had passed. He had his dog with him and walked through his field. His dog often ran off chasing rabbits or the odd pheasant but this time it stood in the field barking. "What's up mate?" the farmer said. "What you found?" He looked down and saw what looked like an arm with a clenched fist. He opened the fist and saw the brooch with its red shiny jewel. "We must get help," he said and rang his brothers. They were close by in a shed.

"What's up?"

"Someone's buried here; we need to get them out." The brothers dug around and dragged her out. Her lungs suddenly took in a deep breath and she coughed and spluttered. She was alive.

"My friend, where is he?" she said. They could not see anyone.

"Better get the fire brigade," they said, "and some diggers."

The authorities spent the whole day clearing the soil and reached the tunnel. "There's nothing here," they said. They even sent cavers down the tunnels, but her friend was never found. She never knew what happened to him. Did he survive? Had he gone back to the start?

As she sat there now at her desk with the small brooch in front of her she wondered if she had dreamt it. Hundreds of creatures rescuing her in an underground sea. None of which the cavers saw when they went down there. She still wonders what was in her coat pocket when she washed it. It looked like a tiny segmented thing rather like a little leg. Was it from one of the creatures? She would never know.

5 THE GOLDEN TONGUE

The little man was not getting younger, all his friends were married and said he must get a wife. He was very shy and every time he went to talk to a girl he changed his mind and walked away his voice was very small and even if he talked to them they could not hear. A man should love before he dies. His best friend's wife had a sister a strong minded muscular woman who rushed round the house checking that things had been done and done correctly. His best friend said, "I've just the person for you, you need to do more than just dream, your worries are over and you will never hesitate again." The little man actually fancied the little ginger haired waitress who was always dressed in black but he decided to meet his friend's wife's sister.

His friend drove him out to a site called the awesome wonder which looked over a valley between mountain pasture. Sitting on a chair in a café was a large girl.

Her long black hair tied tightly on top in a bun so tight that the creases on her forehead were taken out. He wondered how on earth she had managed to do it. She had a white jumper, the sleeves too long and reaching over the back of her hands. Must be cold he thought.

 But it was summer.

"This is flora," his best friend said. They shook hands it was one of those handshakes that feels as if they don't really want to shake hands cold and clammy with a loose grip. Oh, cold hands warm heart he thought. He looked closely at her. Her eyes were grey, she didn't seem that young, and she had a white veil loosely over the top of her head. Her fingers were gnarled it looked as if she had shaven her eyebrows and had once tried to redraw them but they were taking a long time to grow back. She had lost some hair and her hair looked whiter than it actually was. Her skin was like frail netted parchment. She had a tattoo at the back of her neck but he could not make out what it was. On her head she wore sunglasses which reflected the morning white clouds passing by

His friend did most of the talking and they arranged a date, then she left with his friend.

The day came when he was to meet her. At the site was a large yew tree 30ft wide. It was still alive and hollow inside and to his surprise inside sat four men at a table drinking. He greeted them. "How's ye?" they shouted. "Come and join us."

He said, "Sorry, I'm meeting someone.

"Bets it's that Flora," they shouted. The little man wondered how they knew he was meeting her but saw that one of the people at the table was his friend. "Best not to associate you with her," one of the men shouted.

 His friend said, "Shut up."

 "She's got a sharp tongue that lass and beware if you ever cross her she's someone who at night would crawl up to your face and suck out the breath." They laughed and carried on drinking. The little man looked for his date but she had gone. Must have heard what they said he thought and went home. Over the next few weeks he met her with his friend and his wife and after many meetings they agreed to marry. He was not in love with her but she was looking for someone as he was and neither were getting any younger. What was a bit disconcerting was that her parents were country folk and held many strict traditions and beliefs from the past.

Her parents lived in a house with whitewashed inside walls covered in drawings. Over the door was a lintel of joggled stones which he had never seen before. Their house was high up on the side of a mountain. They had been there all their lives and the high altitude pressure meant that their body tissues in arms and legs were quite swollen. They loved to burn perfume which made him cough every time he visited they even believed that all the mishaps that occurred to them or their daughter were put down to demons. They did make nice biscuits though they baked them twice to make them crisp and wrapped them in greaseproof paper. They also produced the best cheese in the area made from cow's milk where the cows fed on the flower meadows. The man also heard that in their family, as with his wife they were all born with two small bumps on their heads caused by pooling of blood. They said people believed they were devil's horns but they soon disappeared.

At the start of his marriage with his wife she was all sweetness and calm but she soon became dominating often screeching out orders and picking on his every action.

People round knew this they could hear her shouting and saw the sadness in his watery blue eyes.

His friend came to see him. What the matter?" he said.

"I've married a monster." He thought of the little ginger girl in the café.

 "I bet she's not a monster."

 Sometimes he would escape and go into the café for a coffee just to see her. His wife was getting violent. One day she threw a huge metal pot at him cutting his face. His neighbour treated it with a paste made out of mouldy bread which she had kept in the rafters of her house. It worked and soon healed up.

It all happened suddenly one Monday morning, the sky turned from bright blue to bright golden yellow. It was as if the sun had spread across the sky. Everyone was talking about it and shielding their eyes from the brightness. Even the sun could no longer be seen against this bright back ground.

Then suddenly, for hundreds of miles as far you could see, a yellow gold dust covered the fields. Cars were covered, cows were covered. The little man was outside; his hat was now yellow with the dust. He called his wife but there was no reply.

"I think we better leave and find out what it is!" he shouted. She heard but he did not take any notice and stayed inside, oblivious to what was happening. The roads were golden yellow. Many cars had stopped and many people were afraid to get out. A radio broadcast said they had no idea what was happening, perhaps it was like the sand that often came down from the Sahara desert. Many said it was global warming, pollution, or the start of the sixth extinction.

It was strange to see birds flying past; they were yellow, just like canaries. Finally there was a huge bang the sky was full of lightning and thunder rolled around the hills. The little man's wife came out of the house and saw that everything was yellow and screamed, "Why didn't you tell me?" But the little man was not there, he had left long ago. She walked out of the back door and slipped on the wet yellow dust and knocked her head and lay at the back of the house unconscious. People were coming out, the sky was now as black as soot and thunder and lightning raged outside.

After a day the little man returned to his home but he could not find anyone he shouted but there was no answer he heard singing coming from the back garden. "Tra la la la la la," he heard. What on earth, he thought. He looked out and saw his wife covered in yellow dust dancing around the garden.

"She's flipped and gone mad," he thought. "I better get out who knows what she might do." But before he could say Jack Robinson she was inside hugging and kissing him and showering him with praise and kind words. He didn't trust her at first but then found she had changed completely. Was it the yellow dust or the fall when she hit her head on the porch? He would never know. Time passed and she remained one of the nicest and kindest persons in the town. She would always praise everyone and soon became known as the little man's wife with the golden tongue. Many others in the town also changed their character but they did not fall and hit their heads so maybe the yellow dust did have some effect after all.

6 THE LITTLE WHITE STOOL

For years it had sat behind the piano stool. On occasion it was taken out for a small child to sit on but most of the time it stayed in place as the years trundled on. It was used to hearing the wonderful sound of great musicians, Beethoven, Bach and the waltzes of Strauss as well as sing along songs from the past. The families would gather round for a good sing song led by an uncle or aunt but now the piano lay quiet, unplayed, gathering dust on its keys, the occupants of the home had long gone and the house was waiting to be sold. The uncle had spent a long time overseas working in an embassy in South Africa before they moved to this house.

Much of the contents of the house, including several foreign relics, had gone already to relatives who popped in and out trying to hold on to personal belongings and memories of past times but those items too would be lost in the sea of life sitting on a shelf somewhere until given to a charity shop disconnected from those who once handled and enjoyed it.

The mirror in the hall no longer reflected the happy faces of the previous occupants but just reflected the light that shone through the porch window every morning. The old aunt who died had loved this mirror and would tidy her hair and sprig herself up before leaving the house.

The house had now been sold and it was time for house clearance. A large skip was put in the drive and one could see the men carrying out objects and throwing them into it. Some large furniture items were smashed so that they would take up less space. The little white wooden stool was so small they just threw it straight in.

A family who were very poor were passing by and saw the men at work. The little girl who was with them peered over the edge of the skip surprised to see broken china and other household items just thrown there like rubbish. "Look mummy, there's a little white stool, don't let them smash that."

The mother said, "It's not ours dear it, belongs to these men now."

One of the men clearing heard her. "Let her have it," he said. "It's only going to be burnt; we've no use for it." So the mother leant over the skip and took it out. The little girl was so pleased she shouted out, "My stool, it's my stool, all mine. Thank you, thank you. I will never throw you away."

Although small the little white stool was quite heavy. Her mother helped her and soon they reached their house. It was only a one bedroom house. The roof needed repairing and the ceilings were damp. Several of the windows had broken and were patched up with tape. It was hard to keep warm in the winter and draughty. They all sat round the fire in the front room and often burned newspapers and magazines to keep warm. The small backyard was full of rubble and weeds. She put the stool in the front room and sat on it next to the old table to play.

They had a big dog. He really was too big for such a small house and cost a lot to feed which they really could not afford. They were given it as a small puppy and the family loved it but they did not realise how big it would grow. They had to take it out twice a day to run in the field next to the house. The father came home one day and decided that the dog must go. They often had little to eat after buying food for the dog and the parents were tired of repairing things the dog had damaged. "I'm sorry he must go to a new home," the mother said to the little girl. The little girl was very upset and ran to her room in tears. All that evening she just lay on her bed with the dog talking to it and crying. The mother tried to persuade her husband to think again but he was angry and said, "No, "and stomped out of the house. The dog's home was contacted and would pick the dog up the next day at 10.am. The mother and the girl decided to take the dog out for a last walk before it was taken away. They put on its lead and made their way to the park where it always loved thrashing around in the dead leaves to find its ball. The little girl hoped it would run off as it would be better than giving it to the dogs' home where she knew many unwanted dogs especially if old and big were put down. But he didn't run away and they brought him back home. As they opened the front door the dog came rushing in as he usually did and this time he knocked over the little stool. To the little girl's surprise the stool did not fall over but rose up on one of its sides as if balanced. Her mother saw it and said. "Why it's like one of those eagles you buy which can balance on its nose. It's all to do with the centre of gravity but I don't know why the stool is behaving in that way." They lifted it up and the mother could feel it was heavier on one side. "That's funny," she said. "It's the same piece of wood used on each side therefore the balance should be in the middle of the stool." She ran her hand over the heavy side and felt a small indent. She put her nail in it and a thin piece of wood rather like the sliding lid on a wooden pencil case moved across. "Why it's got a compartment," she said. "There's something shiny in it."

They tipped the little stool over and a rectangular block of very heavy metal fell out onto the carpet. The mother picked it up and wiped the dirty surface clean with the edge of her skirt. "It's shiny," the little girl said. "It's got writing on it." The mother looked closely. "Wow, it's a gold ingot; the owner must have hid it in here at some time."

The family got it valued and it was worth several thousands of pounds.

"We'll keep that dog," the father said. "We would not have found it if he hadn't knocked that stool over They decided to use the money from the gold to make repairs on their house and sell it. Surprisingly, as it was in London, it was worth a lot of money. They moved down to Kent where they could buy a bigger house with a huge garden for the same price and the father was able to get a better job. The little stool now stands proudly in their front room in the centre of a large table with a beautiful bunch of flowers in a pot on top of it.

7 THE WEDDING DRESS

Once upon a time there was a young woman just about to get married. She had been a delicate child, had a small thin face and upturned nose, long brown hair and a lovely smile.

She was one of those people who could never make up her mind or make a decision on anything. It took her a long time to decide when to get up in the morning and when to go to bed at night what to eat, where to go and how to do things.

She had a boyfriend who had asked her to marry him but she hesitated said no said yes and no again. Finally she decided, persuaded by her mother and sister, to say yes.

But she needed a wedding dress so she went to the shop in the city which had the most choice of dresses, celebrities, politicians and kings and queens had bought dresses at this shop

Ding went the bell on the door as she entered the shop. An experienced dressmaker met her. "What can I help you with?

! I'm getting married in a few weeks' time and I need a dress, something feminine and modern. Something spectacular and stunning so that my husband and guests will say wow but something a bit irrational like me."

"Do you know what kind of dress you are after?" the young woman said.

"No can I see some dresses?"

The first dress which came out was a Cinderella ball gown. "It's a real princess dream dress said the dressmaker, but the girl said, "No I'm at a wedding not a ball!"

"Oh," well said the dressmaker and went back into the store.

"How about this angel dress?" The dress had numerous shreds of material around the base and long silky sleeves.

"It's too bright," she said. "I'm not in heaven yet! I need something fairy tale eye-catching a dress that would conquer the world."

Out came a snow white dress, "It's a beautiful an eye catching fairy tale dress," said the dressmaker. It has a turtle neck."

"No, no," shouted the young woman. She was getting quite upset at not knowing what she would like. Next came a dress with ruffles at the bottom. "Flamenco," the dressmaker said.

"Looks like cut up pieces of paper. I don't want it." She tried on many other dresses even some in red and blue but still could not decide. The dressmaker was so fed up she called the deputy manager to take over.

H hello dear," he said. "Not found what you are looking for?

"No," said the young woman. "There must be something here for me," and she broke down in tears which ran all down her face.

"Now stop that crying now," said the deputy manager. "Remember when you find the right dress it will just happen, just like love. That magic moment. The time when you find the most unique dress to wear for that single special day. "I know exactly what you need," and went to the very back of the store. "Something that will make you feel prettier."

The young woman sat patiently waiting. He came out with a dress that sparkled in the light as if covered with diamonds. "This is our new creation," he said.

"It's a mermaid dress with sweetheart neckline it is made from stands of golden thread."

The young woman had never seen anything like it. She smiled. "Can I try it? Oh please, I have never worn a golden dress before." After a few minutes she appeared. All the staff in the shop gathered round many had not seen such a dress before. Her long golden train flashed with the room lights. "It's fantastic," they all said. "Nobody could not like it. It must be very expensive."

Just then there was a bang and the shop door swung open. It was the manager. "What's going on here?" he said. "Why is that dress out? It's reserved for the countess. She's coming in for a final fitting this afternoon that's why I am here. The jaws of all the staff dropped. The dress was not to be presented to customers it had been specially made.

The young woman on hearing this screamed and fell to the ground. "This can't be true. This is the dress I've always been dreaming of; it's a Goldilocks' dress. She got up suddenly and to everyone's amazement suddenly raced to the door. Some of the staff tried to stop her but she hit out at them, she swung the door open and ran into the main street which was full of shoppers and traffic. She pushed past the people who on seeing her in the dress stopped and stared startled to see a woman in such a beautiful dress. They moved aside thinking she was on her way to her wedding. The shop assistants had left the shop and were pursuing her. "Stop her someone," they shouted. People were taking pictures on their phones and posting them on the internet. And soon the films were shown on local and even international news. Eventually the staff caught up with her and pulled her into a department store to change into her clothes which they had brought with them.

"We're so sorry," they said, and they left her in tears and sitting on the floor. She eventually walked home and flopped herself on the bed. She had no wedding dress and her wedding was in a few days. She would have to wear her mother's old dress but that was much too small.

But that was not the end of the story as pictures of her in the dress were circulating the internet and everyone was amazed at this golden dress. Orders poured into the shop for similar dresses and other dresses. More profit was made in a week than in a year. The manager was delighted if she hadn't run down the street in this dress then this wouldn't have happened. He rang the countess and explained the situation. She was not in a hurry for her dress as she was not getting married until six months later as her fiancé would return from overseas then.

The young woman was at home with her mother sewing pieces of material into the mother's dress to make it bigger when there was a knock on the door. "Miss Matthews?" the man said "Yes I'm Mrs Matthews." He handed her a large box. "What is this? the mother said. "Just sign here please. She did so and brought it inside. They opened it and to their surprise there it was the golden wedding dress with a note. It said. "Truly many thanks for publicising our dresses. We have decided to give you this dress free of charge please try it on and bring it in for a fitting sometime. The young woman put it on and the whole room lit up." This is the dress I chose," she said to her mother. "It just happened suddenly just like falling in love I fell for the dress, this beautiful fairy tale dress.

8 I AM WHITE APHID

I scrambled endlessly through a forest of hairs, up and down, no way of getting out and no idea which way I should go. The strange smell of sweat and soap blocked my senses. I felt the pull as the electrostatic forces acted on my tiny body and tried to push me away. The hairs on the owner's arms varied in colour from black to grey and crisscrossed. Some were very long.

I slowly moved across dark and light patches of skin speckled with freckles and small cuts from a cat or rose bush. Some hairs I climbed up reflected light and shone silvery as I passed across the owner's skin. The odd ginger hair grew here but it was from another younger era of this person's life.

On and on I crawled with no end in sight. The hairs were endless in all direction. At last I reached a hairless old wart. I rested and tried to spread my tiny wings but they had not fully developed yet and were still in their natal coverings. It was very humid on this arm but that was good, I would not dry out. In places there were tiny crystals of salt on the skin which were absorbing water. Also in places there were layers of loose skin scales, the stuff of dandruff and house hold dust. Thank goodness there were no dust mites to encounter on my journey. When would I get off or would I continually struggle and die in this forest of hairs dried up like a raisin? I was so thirsty I had no sap to suck and my mouth parts couldn't pierce the skin like a mosquito.

What if the person felt the movement of a hair caused by my attempts to escape and scratched the arm or even washed it under a tap and wiped it with a towel? That would be the end, as a small, tiny, white aphid I would exist no more. A small insignificant life not loved by anything and little time to feel and respond to the experiences of life itself. Would I have the experience of being carried around by ants who fed on my honey dew that shot out from my siphons on my back?

Fortunately I had no inkling of the constant dangers that continually challenged my relatives on roses, runner beans, or apple branches. Neither did I know about the constant slaughter of my kind by ladybirds and song birds or sly parasitic wasps that could hatch inside me and eat out my insides. Even worse, the garden spray that could paralyse my relatives. But what did that matter. The time was now and I must struggle with every bit of strength I still had from the resources given to me by my mother. I needed to find a food source and develop, in order to prolong the existence of my species on this fragile earth.

There was no chance of survival even if I did get off this hairy arm. I was inside a home, a sitting room with furnishings. I would only fall onto the red carpet which had even more erect hair like fibres. Then there would be no escape as I would be walking on this endless red desert.

But what is this? Something is happening. A small piece of white paper lies in front of me. I am dazzled by its brightness but I will crawl slowly onto it. I am sitting on the edge of it afraid to move as the paper is now moving. I feel a waft of air through my antennae then the sudden noise of chimes as a door is opened. A huge blast of air and bright golden sunlight greets me. Help! I'm being tilted sideways and the paper I stand on is being shaken up and down. I hang on but lose my footing. I'm falling down into darkness. Its moist here, I'm standing on wet soil and above me I can see green which could mean food.

Above me I see the piece of paper being screwed up and the owner tossing it to the ground and hear the bang of the kitchen door being closed. I'm outside and next to a plant. Above me I can see my relatives merrily sucking away at tender new stalks. Up I climb, my life begins at last.

The owner returns to his chair to continue his crossword. His hairy arm moves forward with a pen in his hand. The final clue, six across, a five letter word, garden plant sucking pest- aphid he writes. Crossword complete.

9 A LETTER TO LADY ELLHORN

THE CRONE IN THE ELDERBERRY TREE

Quote

Before taking wood from the elderberry tree one must say:

"Old woman give me some wood and I'll give thee some of mine when I grow into a tree."

DEAR READER

Some call me the lady's tree, elder Hyldemoer, mother figure of all woodlands, goddess of death and regeneration. You may not know me but I dwell in the elder trees. My soul is bound into the life force of this tree and in every tree around the world. I have been revered for years even in megalithic times when long barrows held flints made in the shape of my leaves which were placed in them in funerals. If you find me I will always be close to humans and will protect those who care for me.

Most humans from the beginning of time have come to know that taking any part of my tree will bring bad luck unless something is given in return. Even a prayer. As I grow I am transformed and cross the threshold between life and death. Even lightning dare not strike me.

Woe to those who have not asked for my wood to make furniture, musical instruments, even floorboards. If a child is put in a cradle made from my wood I'll drag it out by its ankles and pinch it black and blue until it shrieks. Just break one of my twigs and see what happens. Hedge cutters know too well so avoid me. Using a twig in the past to cane a child stopped its growth.

My flowers' smell repels insects and animals, a cat like smell and no plant grows under its spell. I do not burn well and can in anger release my spirit along with fumes of noxious cyanogen glycosides.

 Elder is the lady's tree burn it not or cursed be ye.

My branches shoot out on opposite sides giving a cross like appearance. Some say my wood was used to make the cross that Jesus died on.

Bour tree crooked trung
Never straight and never strong
Never bush and never tree
Since our lord was nailed on thee.

If you look at my branches they grow vertical then hang down caused by the weight of Judas who hanged himself on one of my trees. My stems are hollow, full of pith. Anglo Saxons used these hollow stems to blow up flames in a fire. In the middle ages on Christmas Eve they cut discs of my pith, coated each in oil, floated them on water and set them alight to ward off evil spirits.

Remember to wear my twigs at weddings for good luck or as a headdress then you will see my spirit. Branches in or outside your house can protect against evil. Some put them in coffins or put my twigs in a cross on graves. My stems can be used as the strongest wands to summon spirits. Close your eyes under my tree and you could stay in fairy land for ever.

Just like the Druids you can make wine from my berries, even champagne today but beware .my berries have magical powers especially on mid summer's eve. They can be dried and put around your neck for protection but eat them raw off my tree and I will see that they make you vomit and give you diarrhoea.

Do you want to see your Lady of the elderberry? Just bathe your eyes with the green juice of my leaves.

You can't kill me easily every part of my stems and shallow roots regenerate and grow rapidly. Put a cutting in the ground and it lasts longer than iron. Stick one of my stems in a grave and see if it grows. If it flowers the occupant is at peace, if it dies they are in hell.

Beware if my shadow falls on your house. You're likely to die young. Bakers plant me near their house to prevent the devil being folded in with the bread dough.

Many today agree that my fruits and flowers and foliage have healing powers. A wonderful medicine chest for wounds and respiratory disorders and a diuretic and emetic

Don't fret if I die. I am the spirit of transformation from death to life. My spirit remains inside every seed in every berry.

Why not today put a leaf in your pocket for protection? Throw my leaves to the wind and shout out loud the name of those you wish to bless or scatter leaves over them.

But just remember to get my permission if you want to take any part of me in the future or else I will take revenge!

YOURS SINCERELY

LADY ELLHORN

10 'I'M COMING FOR YOU NOW'

The shop was crowded. Upstairs there were all the Christmas decorations splendidly arranged in their resplendent colours. On the displays were tinsel with fluorescent colours, and every shape and form of bauble you could imagine in plastic, wood or glass. Large nodding dwarf like figures with long beards stood proudly in rows while small Santas stood in rows dressed in their winter furs. Artificial trees stood proud and straight covered in powdered snow, sparkle or lights while the usual stockings and tree accessories also were now on display. It was only October but the shop needed to sell the goods as they had over ordered this year.

This dazzling array of sparkle cheered the customers especially as the days were getting shorter and darker earlier.

Round the corner from the Christmas display was the Halloween display. This year every gruesome imaginable form of horror was on display from skeletons to witches, pumpkin headed reapers, and tortuous figures that moved and screamed, "let me out," or cackled.

Poor clowns, once seen as happy, friendly figures of fun and laughter by children, were now defined as something horrible with nasty smiles and darkened eyes. This was all because of some bad publicity and horror films where the writers ran out of ideas to shock people. Times had changed, a clown or a man talking to a child or rescuing it from a disaster would now be labelled a paedophile.

Anyhow, hidden amongst the halloween makeup and spiders' webs on the bottom shelf were hollow, plastic, golden orange pumpkins. Dialling a number on the front would turn on a red light inside and make a telephone on its head ring. On lifting the receiver one could get a reply. A deep voice bellowed out loudly, "I'm coming for you now; I'll see you in the grave." Words not very reassuring for the easily frightened or elderly person close to death's door.

Moving on I returned to pass down a covered corridor which had a Christmas display. Wired deer were covered in lights. Some were not made out of wires but formed from linked plastic jewels also lit up but more expensive than the wire forms of cable lights. On each side of the darkened corridor were examples of animated scenes. Small lit up containers with glitter of gold or silver could be seen the flake in water over a Christmas figure. There were Christmas roundabouts with children on, and skiers continuously skiing down slopes. Also there were ferris wheels and figures of Santa in his sleigh and his reindeer rising and falling over some plaster houses. Many scenes were like old Victorian ones lit up with small trains moving in circles or people dressed in costume revolving on small podiums. There were also lanterns or even television like boxes with polystyrene snow blown up and falling onto model trees, Santa and snowmen. For the newcomer and children this must have been something captivating especially at this time now before some inquisitive child had started to destroy some of the scenes often leaving only wires exposed. As I reached half way down this isle I heard a voice coming from over the top of the display, "I'm coming for you now; I'll see you in the grave." Oh, I thought, someone must have dialled that pumpkin so I went round to see but there was no one in sight.

 They must have left, but on returning to the Christmas displays there was the voice again. Once again I returned to the Halloween section but still there was no one there. Oh they must have put some sort of link through to this section I thought or it was just activated by noise somewhere and thought nothing of it. That was until I left the shop.

It was dark and raining and I had other things on my mind and forgot all about it. Next day I went back to the shop to see if it had automatic sound but it hadn't. "You need to dial the golden pumpkin's phone to activate it," the shop assistant said.

It was 10.30 and I again went through the Christmas corridor with all its fancy lit up displays and I heard it again. I ran around quickly to see if anyone had pressed the button but there was no one there.

I left and went back to work and forgot about the whole thing until the next day. I looked at my watch; it was 10.30 I suddenly felt as though my head was spinning and felt a pain in my arm. When I opened my eyes I was back in the Christmas corridor this time the voice seemed to be booming out," I'll see you in the grave." But how could that be? I had gone to work. I found myself back at work and in a panic asked my colleagues if I had gone out and they said I had been there all the time. I must have dreamt it I thought, must have dozed off. I sometimes did. But no, the same situation occurred the next day. I even set up a video recorder to film me at 10.30 but there I was busily working at my desk. It was like a routine which becomes embedded in someone's behaviour just as the hands of a clock reach the same point every twelve hours. Was it a foreboding? Was I to die or was something evil haunting me?

I went to the doctor who gave me some antidepressants which seemed to calm me down but I felt I was at the edge of a breakdown. I tried to occupy myself with other things at the 10.30 slot but still I returned to the Christmas corridor. I must sort this I thought, so I took a friend with me to the shop at the same time we went up the escalator but saw that the Halloween goods were gone. Halloween was over now. But at the bottom of one of the racks there still was a golden pumpkin, its sides a bit battered.

Perhaps I should buy it so as to reassure me the sound only came from this silly man made toy. I went over to the shop assistant who came over to see what I was looking at. "Not working." he said, "We are not allowed to reduced it or sell it. We'll have to dump it. Sorry you can't have it." It was always a pain going off in the mornings until the battery ran out. That's it, that's it, I thought that glitch in my life was a faulty toy. I laughed and walked out with my friend. I looked at my watch it had gone 10.30. Nothing to worry about, but suddenly I felt a pain in my arm and once again found myself in the Christmas corridor but there was no, "I'm coming for you now; I'll see you in the grave," only a large smiling Santa rocking to and fro singing 'We wish you a merry Christmas, we wish you a merry Christmas, we wish you a merry Christmas and a happy new year.'

I was trapped again in a moment of time, a Christmas déjà vu. Did other people have this over the rainbow experience? Yes, I found out. Others did, trapped in different time loops like a display video. I was not alone. In the store they were taking down the

Christmas decorations. The Christmas corridor had gone. I was free now or was I? I had to wait and see.

11 BISCUIT MAN

Samuel's family had always been into biscuits. His mother had worked in a biscuit factory while his father had a grocery shop full of different kinds of biscuits on display in large metal tins. They even had a sign on the shop advertising one kind of biscuit. But now sadly that had all disappeared. The shop had closed after his father's death and the factory had now become automated. There was only one thing for it said Samuel his son. I will go to Australia and seek my fortune. He managed to get on a cargo ship, but the voyage took many months and his health suffered. He was suffering from scurvy and to his horror lost two of his front teeth. When finally they reached Australia he could hardly walk and in a daze stumbled off the ship carrying the few belongings that he had.

Over the road at the dock there was a small church. He managed to crawl through the door and sat on one of the pews inside.

It was a very old church and had seen better times. There were holes in the roof and the windows and many of the pews were broken. There were also people sleeping on some of them. Suddenly there was a loud clanging noise. Someone was hitting a piece of rusty steel with a metal rod. Samuel looked up. "Come and get it," a woman shouted. The bodies on the pews rose up as if resurrected and trundled slowly toward a solid wooden door at the side of the church. Samuel got up and followed

They entered a small room with a corrugated roof. There were long tables scattered about with some chairs, but the others used old petrol drums. He could smell something. It was stew. They were going to be given something to eat. He walked in and found a large woman who said, "Plate please over there." He reached over and grabbed a metal plate. She smiled.

"Hold it out." He did so and a large helping of lamb stew flopped onto his plate. "There's bread over there," she said. He moved away so as to let the others behind him move forward. He ambled over to a table where there was a pile of spoons in the middle. He took one and sat at one end.

"That's his seat," those at the table shouted. He moved to another table and again was shunted away. There was a small table in one corner which used to be a card table but most of the green felt had worn off and was moth eaten, the light plywood underneath was stained with old drink. At least he had a chair but he soon realised it was a bit rickety so he tried not to lean back too much. Someone came towards him. It was a woman of small stature with flowing ginger hair tied at the back. He half expected her to say it was someone else's seat but she didn't .She said, "Anyone sitting there?" Samuel said no so she went over and fetched an empty petrol drum and sat on it next to him.

"I'm Gillie," she said. Some call me Gill as I often go fishing with my brother. Samuel was hungry so got on with his stew not really needing to be interrupted by this chatty person. Gill started eating too. "You're new here?" she said. "Haven't seen you here before." Samuel tried to cover his mouth so she wouldn't see that he had lost two front teeth.

"No, I just came off a ship. I'm looking for work. Do you know if there is any?

"Not much around here," she said. "It's dead. Used to be a thriving fishing port but it was taken over by the large docks further up the coast. There are no jobs here. You'll have to go into town. Samuel thanked Gillie and left her finishing off her stew which she ate very slowly. He got onto a bus to get off at the nearest town. It was very hot and dusty. The windows of the bus were covered in fine red dust which blew up from the back as the bus sped on. He got off at the edge of what looked like a town. It was quite desolate with only two stores. He went into a bar and sat at a table. A man came over to him.

"Do you know if there are any jobs here," Samuel said.

"Plenty of manual work in the main city," he said. But Samuel could not do this as he had injured his arm fighting in the army.

"Sorry mate, nothing else."

Some scruffy men with leather brown hats sat at a table in the corner. They had heard him asking.

"How about joining us? Have you ever heard of the Golders then that's us. We look for gold in the old areas where the mines were. We could do with an extra pair of hands; one of our mates has just left us to spend more time with his family. It's hot work though all day out in the bush, that's why we've got these big hats. One day well strike it lucky and find a stash of gold and won't have to work again."

Samuel was not sure. They sounded crazy. "Have you found much gold?" he asked.

"Enough to cover our costs," they said. "This year we've got a permit on a site next to where a sixteen year old found a nugget shaped like an eagle, the largest gold nugget ever found. If you're interested stand outside this pub at six and we'll pick you up."

Samuel nodded and went over to get a drink. The men left and Samuel booked a room above the pub. He wasn't sure he would wake up that early, but he knew they had an early start as it would get hotter as the day went on. That evening he went downstairs to get a meal. He was surprised to see Gillie over at another table laughing and joking with a man. He wondered if she worked there, but he faced away not wanting to attract her attention. The meal was large and very filling. He had a few drinks and was just about to get up when Gillie noticed him and came over. Blast he thought, she's going to chat me up.

"Hi, you're the one with the missing teeth?" Samuel cringed and quickly covered his mouth.

"So this is how far you've got. Got a job yet?

"Nope," he said.

"Come and join me."

He said "I've got to get up early tomorrow I'm going gold hunting."

She burst into laughter. "Mugs game There's not much gold around here. People have been searching for years but not found any. The old timers really stripped this place of any gold. This is my brother."

Samuel shook his hand, "See you around," he said and got up.

"If you must go," she said.

It was 6 am and Samuel, half asleep, struggled out of the pub onto the High Street. There was an old battered truck outside its engine struggling to keep going. "Jump in the back," said the driver. They picked up two other men and to his surprise Gillie's brother was there. "Can't miss this opportunity," he said. "You green horn may bring us luck." They drove out far into the bush over stony tracks.

"We've got you a detector," the boss said. "Not much cop, it's old and it will give scream out if you find something. Here's a chain. Tie it to your belt at the back so it drags on the ground and you can see where you've already been."

It was quite heavy and he could feel it pulling his belt away from his trousers.

He worked with the others and soon got a sound. One of three men came over and got a pick and removed the top soil. He then put his detector over the spot to see if it was still at the spot. Samuel then dug. He was quite excited, his first gold, it might be huge. But he was less so when the man said, "look, it's just an old bullet case. There are lots of these around from when they hunted game. There's also shoe nails and odd scraps of metal. That's the name of the game. Keep searching."

Samuel spent the whole season with them. They all found gold enough to cover their costs and make some profit. The boss decided to give up the plot at the end of the year and try elsewhere. "Want a plot?"

he said to Samuel. Samuel knew he had not covered the whole area and after some time he decided he would give it a go and rented it for a season putting marker poles plus paper work in each corner. They gave him the detector he had used, saying there was not much life left in it so he might as well have it.

He was excited and made ready for the next season. Before he started he went back to the port where he had arrived and went into the church to see if Gillie was still there. He was told she had not been around for weeks and the priest in charge said she was very ill and living with her sister. Samuel decided to go and see her. Her sister's place was dark and dismal. The curtains inside were dirty and torn and the furniture was in a very bad state. He was offered tea from some small tin mugs. He could see they were very poor.

For two weeks Samuel went to visit, each time bringing food and wood for the fire. As the weeks went by Gillie gradually recovered. In the meantime Samuel was out detecting on his plot. He had some luck, but the gold was just tiny pieces worth only a few dollars. Minerals around the gold amplified the signal making the beeps louder as one would expect for a larger find. He had to be careful in places as old, very deep mineshafts were concealed and he could easily lose his footing and fall down one. He wondered how the old timers managed with only a candle.

Gillie now had fully recovered and Samuel invited her to come prospecting. She remembered her grandfather had looked for gold and even went underground. She also remembered how he would say gold is often washed down into river beds and along water courses. She said to Samuel "You'll know if gold is washed down as the nuggets will have smooth edges."

There was a lot of gravel on the ground and they thought it might be a river bed. There was a beep then another.

"It's a honey hole!" Gillie shouted. Lots of nuggets were close together. They were excited but still the pieces were very small.

For days they searched in the hot sun with no results. Then on one Friday morning, it had just rained and their luck changed. The gold they found was spiky not smooth. Gillie said they may have hit an old reef where bits of gold are split off from an original source. They were now finding large pieces and even found spongy gold which was worth more. Every day they found more and more gold and made a great deal of money.

Gillie, with some of the profits helped her sister find a new place to live and Samuel gave a lot of funds to the church. He rented a site near his last plot which also had a lot of gold and bought machinery to dig and extract gold from the soil.

With his riches he set up a small factory making biscuits like his family had been involved in back at home. The biscuits were rectangular in shape and had the words 'gold finders' inscribed on top of each one. They became very popular.

He would give packets of the biscuits to the poor and would every month include a small flattened biscuit-shaped piece of gold in the packet for them. Soon people heard about this so Samuel decided to include the chance of finding this sliver of gold in the packs he sent to the cities. His lucky biscuits made him a very rich and popular man. He married Gillie and both were great benefactors for the country.

Everybody he met greeted him as the biscuit man. He would smile and point to his two front teeth. Golden teeth, shining in the sun. No longer did he need to hide the fact that he had lost his own.

12 LEFT BEHIND

I remember my mother, half termite half human. She lived in darkness in a huge cavern under her royal palace, Battersea Power Station. She was surrounded by hundreds of workers, servants who saw to her every need. They had to as she was a huge bloated sac with a small head and reduced limbs and could only move her large body in ripples from her front to her back. But she was revered by all and controlled us all with her chemical messages she spread throughout the colony. She was a magnificent feat of nature an egg laying machine often producing eggs at the rate of one every few seconds.

I remember my large flying brothers and sisters. They were all packed like sardines in small chambers near the base of the chimneys ready to fly up and out of the top. I was outside when they had their maiden flight from their dark prisons. The sky was black with them and I watched them fly in formation over the top of Buckingham Palace like a ceremonial fly pass for the Queen of England.

The palace (Battersea Power Station) was guarded by soldiers, huge soft bodied creatures with enormous heads and curved mandibles that could slice an intruder in half. Many a time had I seen them fight dogs from Battersea Dogs' Home leaving sections scattered all over the concrete car park. As well as protecting our queen they supervised the delivery of massive piles of wood and trees which formed the diet of the occupants inside. There were also other stockpiles all around London so that our foraging parties had resources to continue their pillaging. Roads were full of small round pellets left by these migrants and street sweepers had given up long ago trying to sweep them up. They also feared being decapitated by soldiers. In fact few people roamed the streets these days as many had left to move down to Cornwall or across to Kent where they felt safer.

Looking around London one could see the devastation we had caused when we threated to eat London (see earlier publication Human Termites Eat London) Park benches had gone, gangs descending on them and finishing them off in a single night. Pews in churches also were no longer seen. They had been replaced by plastic chairs said to be useful for removing when they needed the space for events. In some places in the city doors and window frames were missing. Piles of broken glass lay on the ground. Some roof timbers had also disappeared, the upper floors filled with broken tiles.

I remember the day. It was in summer. We could see members of the army running around in Battersea. Our soldiers though had caught some and now in Battersea Park they lay in pieces. It was around eleven. I was outside a fair way from the Battersea Power Station palace when there was an enormous bang and clouds of black smoke filled the London skies. I ran towards the scene only to see the remains of a huge crater where once our majesty had been. A bomb had exploded and she was dead. Soon after there was chaos all around the country as communication had been lost with her majesty and one by one members of our society died. I was left alone. Why didn't I die like the rest? I will never know. But I survived.

Today I am living amongst the true humans. I work in an office 9-5pm as an admin assistant in a genetic research firm well known for genetic editing and trying to find ways of removing genetic defects in humans.

I've finally overcome my appetite for paper .We used to eat tons of it and the outsides of our houses were piled high with old newspapers. As I'm dealing with paper all the time now I concentrate on the contents of the pages not the paper itself. At first I put menthol chest rub over my nose and small antennae to mask the sweet smell of paper but now I don't need it. I must admit though that I do nibble my pencils down to small stubs but nobody notices and there are plenty of pencils in the office. I made sure I had a metal chair and desk so I could not gnaw on them. I've also metal filing cabinets.

I live on my own in a basement flat. It's nice and dark, damp and quite warm down there. Nobody comes inside, the gas and electric metres are outside so I'm safe. The door is triple locked just in case. The walls of all my rooms have been plastered with mud It took a long time to do this and I had to carry buckets full down at night but I finished it and the rooms have a nice earthy smell. Outside the front door, like everyone else in the road, I have a pile of logs but not for burning, just for food. Though I admit I have burnt some when it gets very cold.

I don't eat at work except for a few little wooden chips I carry in my pocket. But when I get home I make up for it. I have a great selection of tasty wooden blocks of all shapes and sizes. Pine and spruce are my favourites and sometimes I have cherry wood and often maple and poplar. I have a large supply ordered on line from China. It seems many are used as children's bricks but even so they are delicious. With the blocks I have found that mashed up cardboard boxes are delicious. One could say they are equal to the mashed potato you humans love so much. I love to nibble down sticks though not bamboos. Wooden broom handles are a luxury as they last so long. Chop sticks and wooden spatulas definitely don't last long. My favourite on a hot summer's day are wood chip lollies. They are packed solid with different kinds of wood in different layers. Delicious. I tried some boat oars once but they were varnished and salty so I gave up on them. Now and then I go on a rampage. My conquests include two bird boxes, a dog kennel (no dog inside) a beer barrel, a chest of drawers and a couple of panels of a fence.Ive been lucky enough to find a hockey stick to devour as well as a few recent novels, a child's cardboard playhouse, even a set of drum sticks. I love polystyrene, not to eat but to chew; my rooms are often full of little pieces. Unfortunately my passion has overridden common sense sometimes. On one occasion while waiting in a queue I ate my theatre tickets so could not get in.

For breakfast before going to work I have also followed a similar habit like humans in that I warm up thick squares of cardboard and cover them with butter and honey and they are delicious, just like your toast and jam. The company I work for says that our queen originated from Africa somewhere and came over to this country to take over from her Majesty the Queen. How true that is I don't know. Perhaps one day they can help me solve my problems and make me truly human not half termite.

Throughout the years I had heard that Battersea Power Station, my queen's old palace, would be reconstructed into amazing new venues by international buyers but this never happened. Now it seems that work is finally underway.

It was a Sunday; the workmen at the old remains of Battersea Power Station were working at the weekend. They had diggers and lorries removing the foundations inside where the queen had once lain. I could hear them commenting when they found the hard parts of some of my past society. "Another blooming mite," they would say. I managed to crawl in under the wire mesh fence. Much of the excavated earth was heaped up on one side. It was wet, probably due to its close proximity to the Thames. I looked at the pile I could see bits of exoskeleton of the soldiers who had done their utmost best to defend this site. To one side I could see a large piece of cuticle, what one called a sclerite. Its edge stuck out of the top. I went over to it and with all my effort pulled it out .It was huge, certainly not from a small member of my family. It's part of the queen I thought to myself. Something to keep hold off, to remember her majesty. But what was this on the underside? It was a layer of cuticle and fat which still looked really fresh. Somehow it had been preserved in this clay river soil. I quickly took off my jacket and wrapped it round it and put it under my arm and made my way out as fast as I could. I ran home excited. My queen, my queen. I threw open my front door and made my way towards my chest freezer. I threw out most of the contents, they didn't really need freezing anyhow and threw the sclerite inside and closed the lid.

I had made quite a few acquaintances at my work, especially scientists who would always come and ask me questions. They knew I was interested in their work. One especially was a bit of a revolutionary. He had always hoped to resurrect some of those animals that existed in the past. He had DNA from frozen mammoths and from bones and teeth of many extinct animals in his freezer. I met him that night in a pub. Although half termite I loved to drink, probably, that was the human side of me coming through, I don't know. I told him about my find and said it might be the queen. His ears pricked up like some animal. "Bring it in," he said. "I'll have a look at it." The next day I took it out of the freezer and wrapped it in bubble wrap and took it into his lab. "Wow, it's huge," he said. "She must have been massive, a real beauty."

"Yes," I said. "An egg laying machine."

I left it with him and went back to work. He rang me at lunch time. "Can we meet up? Exciting news," he said. "I've found some viable DNA from your queen's tissue within the fat. There is quite a bit. I am putting it through the sequencer tonight and we will see what we've got." The next day he came into the office with a long strip of paper. "Look, I sequenced it. These are the arrangement of bases and it shows the differences. Mainly I suspect in morphology and hormonal attributes." I was amazed.

"Can you do anything with it?" I asked.

Jokingly he said, "Well perhaps we can modify the RNA and inject it into someone. But who in their right mind would want to do that. "But it's a good find," he said. "I can write a paper on it. Perhaps we can inject it into an animal?"

The finding of this niggled in my mind all that night and I could not sleep. This was my queen. She was my life and my support. I would have done anything for her. I woke up with a start and a determination of which I seemed to have no control. I left my flat and I burst into my friend's lab. "Inject me," I said.

"You must be joking, it's likely not to work and who knows it might kill you!"

"Do it," I said. "I would rather be dead now than you not do it."

He said, "Ok, if you really insist. I will prepare a very dilute dose to see what slight effect it will have. "

That night I went to his lab. He had prepared the dose on the bench and filled up a small syringe and injected some liquid into my arm. "You'll stay here tonight, that's an order," he said. "I will stay with you in case anything goes wrong and we have to send you to the hospital. Make yourself comfortable and I'll go and make some coffee."

I saw that he had given me very little of the mixture in the vial and I was not satisfied with his caution. I reached over and refilled the syringe with most of the content from the vial and reinjected myself. My friend came in. "You stupid fool," he said. "Who knows what effect that will have? I'm responsible for your safety. I will lose my job if anyone finds out."

"Don't worry," I said. "No one will know and I feel really well."

The night passed. I felt a few murmurs in my stomach but that was probably because I was hungry. The morning came. My friend asked, "Anything happened?" He checked my blood pressure, my temperature and pulse. "Perfectly normal," he said. It had no effect."

"Shame," I said and went into the office to start work

I don't know if it was tiredness from lack of sleep but my head was pounding that morning. I took a few aspirins which seemed to do the trick. I noticed that my hands also seemed a bit pudgy and I felt heavy. I rang work the next morning and I apologised saying I must be coming down with a cold. I feasted on some of my wood chip lollies in the hope they would cool me down. I now definitely had a fever so I slumped myself on my bed and wrapped myself tightly in a blanket hoping to sleep this off. I was awoken by a noise, some high pitched squeaking. I looked across the room and saw two mice were fighting each other. I could hear them really well. Also my alarm clock was ticking louder than I had heard before I could even hear the traffic outside as though it was in the room. It seemed I had heightened hearing how strange. I got up to make a honey cardboard sandwich but found it difficult. My legs and arms were swollen and my heart was beating at an alarming rate. I felt my back was itching and running my hand over it I could feel a line of hard patches along my spine. Gosh, it must be working that injection was changing me. I was afraid really afraid. I was not sure what I would turn into but I had to find a safer place than my house.

I knew from some metal detecting I did several years ago that there was a sewer which was said to be once one of the River Tyburn's outlets to the Thames. It was wet and dark and could be a great place to hide. I took a big canvas bag with me and a lot of wooden blocks and blankets to keep me warm and set out to find the place. It was getting dark. I took a large torch and made my way to the entrance at the side of the Thames. It had a grid over it but could be easily pushed aside. I crept inside. It really stank. It certainly was a sewer but it was quite high and I waded through the shallow water at its base. Suddenly it seemed to branch to the left leaving the main sewer. Here it was dry so I continued on. I just carried on and on hoping it would open out into some sort of chamber in the end. At one point there were steps leading upwards. It's a way out I thought so I went up them. It led to a well-lit tunnel. There were rail tracks. The place was like a mini underground. I suddenly realised I was in the post office railway. This runs under Buckingham Palace. Perhaps that is where I was. There were plenty of side chambers which had not been used for a time and it was warm there. Ideal for me I thought to sit out this metamorphism or whatever it was. There was plenty of discarded paper and boxes to eat and even a wood store. I settled down and went to sleep. I was awoken by voices and two staff members entered and seemed to be loading some mail onto a small train that ran from the palace. They were soon gone.

The days went by and I became more lethargic. It was all I could do to get hold of the food around me. All my wood blocks had been eaten. I heard a voice, it was a girl. She was dressed as a maid and had come down to retrieve some post. I called out. "Help me, please help me," which startled her and she disappeared. About an hour later she returned with a servant and they shone a light on me. I covered my eyes. They gasped in horror at the sight of me but could see my human face on the end of this enormous body which completely filled the chamber. They then disappeared. I heard voices and a lady and young gentleman were standing over me with some of the staff.

"What is it?" I heard the lady say.

"It's a woman; well it's a woman's face, she looks so sad."

"I'll just talk to her," said the lady. And she sat on the edge of a small stone wall. "Who are you?" she asked and I told her the whole story. She remembered how they had had to move out when the human termites threatened London.

"So you're a queen?" she asked.

"It seems so," I said, "But I'm dying here."

"Well we can't have that can we. We must find a more suitable place for you to live. Do you need anything?"

I said, "Some logs would be great."

"Ah well I'll have someone bring some down. So hang on in there. We'll have you out of there in no time."

She was true to her word. I found myself being hoisted up the main stairs through the kitchens in the basement and outside of the palace. A large helicopter was waiting there.

"See she gets to where she belongs," the lady said.

"Certainly your majesty," said the pilot.

I realised then that this was the Queen of England

I shouted, "Your majesty, where are you sending me?"

"Home back to Africa where your mother originated from. Somewhere where you'll be safe and there's plenty of wood and people who can help you survive."

I was grateful and saw her wave goodbye as the helicopter lifted off. I suddenly felt a huge pain then a relief. Another pain and a relief. I twisted my head around only to see two glistening objects in the floor. What are those? I thought and then realised they were eggs. I was egg producing. If they hatched I would have lots of helpers and could build up a large colony. Perhaps one day my children would return to London. This time not to wreak havoc but to work with true humans and make Britain great once again.

To see other publications below by the author visit **snappysnappybooks.com or just search Dr Mike Pearce Amazon books.**

Many of these books in these volumes are also published individually

SNAPPY SNAPPY COLLECTIONS:

Volume 1. BUSINESS AND SELF CONFIDENCE

How to be a Successful Business Weed
Clingers, Creepers and Scramblers
How to Deal with Life's Snakes and Ladders
Trust-Nothing but a Must
Know Your Students and Build Your Image
Hidden from the Heart but not Forgotten
More Pens for Pops
Charity Shops

Volume 2. IDENTITIES, HANG UPS AND CONCERNS
I Herring Gull
Pulvi Royal
I am Termite
Go Fat Go
Make up-Revealed
Fertility Stones and Chocolate Eggs
Captain Grottbuster versus the Grey World
The kittiwakes Warning

Wastefulness-Bone and Urine
Tails, Tales
A slice of Slang with a touch of Cockney and a drop
of Dorset

Mr Hamstrings Dinner

Volume 3. HORROR AND HISTORY

The Living Fossils
My Therizinosaurus
Human Termites eat London
Pigeons Splat London
Glass Anemones Tentacle-ize London
Beware of Cucumbers, Apples and Pigs
The Cornish Urchin
Baby Toes
Googolplex of Mice
Screaming Alley
The Night Mare
Queen Rat on Deadman's Island
Dead Donkey Lane
Old Mother Nature laughed and Laughed
The Plaster Room

Volume 4. RELIGION AND HOPEFULNESS

Pattern for Purpose God's and Man's designs
The Littlest Oyster
Tuppeny Hangover
In a Dark, Dark Corner was the Holy Ghost
The Little Shepherd Boy's Gift
Spider in the Tomb

The Sparrows' Last Soul
The Pawnbroker's Souls
The Red Church Doll
The Boy who found Christmas
The Eggstraordinary Easter Egg
Little Mary
Shepherd's Purse
Sitting next to Angels
The White Lily-St Mildred-Patron Saint of Thanet

Volume 5. TIDE AND TIME

The Shell Man
The Shell Lady
The Watcher on the Fal
The Rock Pool
A Call under the Sea
Pocket full of Starfish
The Scrofula Infirmary
Till my Lips were Salt as Brine
The Man with a Book on his Head
Coloured Bricks
The Girl Under the Paeony Tree
Nothing but Leaves
The China Blackbird
The Man who Collected Figures
The Rusty Gate
Time Runs Dry (a play set in a care home)

Volume 6. FAIRY TALES AND POEMS

The Nursery Rhyme Cat
 Cats at Christmas

The Tuppeny Bear
The Giant and the Giraffe Boy
The Giant's Toothpick
The White Cockerel
The Old Pot and the Golden Shoes
Ball Rooms
Exodus to a Leaf
The Forlorn Fruit Fly
Two Sleepy Boys
Mrs Light and Mr Dark
 I'm Just Going to the Bathroom
The Tulip Tree
The Man who always Sprinted
Bits and Bobs (Poems and short stories for children)

Volume 7. A VARIETY OF WOMEN

Photosynthetic Women
Absorbed by a Woman
The Slothful Wife
Betty's Barcodes
Valentines Cards
The Lady loves Red
The Woman who Smelled Books
Boy, Could She Smell!
The Lady who loved Hairspray

Volume 8. **CHRISTMAS BOOKS**

Impy Christmas
The Little Shepherd Boys Gift
The Boy who found Christmas
Oh, father Christmas what yer going to do?
Nothing but leaves
The Tuppeny hangover
The China Blackbird
The Tuppeny Bear
Cats at Christmas
I Hate Christmas

Volume 9. **HIDDEN PERCEPTIONS**

Silhouette on the pier
I'm not a dinosaur
Mr Mucus
The golden steps
Napoleonic Frankenstein

Volume 10. **MANY CURIOUS STORIES**

The house that cries
The paint brush
The man who collected smiles
Jack and the ivy
The stolen baby
The angels quest
The silly isles
Wilderness Way
I am shadow
The lift

Volume11. CHRISTMAS BOOKS 2
Christmas butterfly
The man in the library
City of laughter, city of tears
Blower Armageddon
Happy Christmas
Antman
A fairy journey
The top of the hill
The Christmas visitor
Ring up an angel
The Christmas raindrop

Volume 12.FAITH AND FAME
Fight for Faith (Gordon of Khartoum)
Angel 1818 (James Blundell)
The Saint who carried his head (St. Denis)

Volume 13. A CORNUCOPIA OF SHORT STORIES
The cursing stone
Punch and Judy (New version)
Touch of Kent dialect
One in 20 million
Be a used seed (Finding new horions)
'Open Arse' (The maligned Medlar)
Wings of colour
Elephant pin-cushion

Volume 14 PLANTASTIC
One in twenty million
Be a seed(Finding new horizons)
The open arse (A maligned medlar)
Nothing but leaves
Exodus to a leaf
The tulip tree
Photosynthetic women
Shepherd's purse
 The girl under the paeony tree
Jack and the ivy
Baby toes
Half a flower
How to be a successful business weed
Clingers creepers and scramblers

Volume 15 INSECTASiA
I am termite
Mother of hundreds
The living fossils
Human termites eat London
Brief encounters with insects
Spider in the tomb
The forlorn fruit fly
The Christmas butterfly
Towers of wax
Antman

Volume 16. TA TA TALES
Condiment kiss
Half a flower
Towers of wax
Gee haw whammydiddle
Peeping Tom
Flowers in the snow
One hundred
Life's escalators
Swallowed by a whale

OTHER STAND ALONE PUBLICATIONS
at snappysnappybooks.com

Red Fred Cell and Friends (Human Biology -
advanced level
Ronnie's Sermon Snippets
Viking Bay-Natural History (Broadstairs, Kent)
The World of Wax
God rest you Merry Scrooge
Napoleonic Frankenstein
Satan's stars

ABOUT THE AUTHOR

Dr Mike Pearce is a scientist interested in behaviour. He also was a lecturer in human biology and health at a college in Canterbury, Kent